BREAKING, NURSING, REPAIRING A BROKEN HEART

CONNOR WHITELEY

No part of this book may be reproduced in any form or by any electronic or mechanical means. Including information storage, and retrieval systems, without written permission from the author except for the use of brief quotations in a book review.

This book is NOT legal, professional, medical, financial or any type of official advice.

Any questions about the book, rights licensing, or to contact the author, please email connorwhiteley@connorwhiteley.net

Copyright © 2023 CONNOR WHITELEY

All rights reserved.

DEDICATION
Thank you to all my readers without you I couldn't do what I love.

PART ONE: BREAKING A HEART

CHAPTER 1
17th June 2022
Canterbury, England

Josh Grant walked on a little narrow path next to a long road with wonderfully green trees lining it as he went towards his university social tonight. He had almost driven down to the university earlier on but it turned out his sense of direction was rather poor.

He parked his car in the only car park he knew that would be open on an early Friday evening, but it turned out it was on the completely opposite end of the campus to where his university social was meant to be.

So he was in for a long old walk.

But at least he had his university social to go to. Something that he was extremely looking forward to.

After a long year as a university placement student, he normally just said to people that he was doing a year of work experience, he was so excited about it all being over and he could finally crack on with his summer.

It was far from the fact that he hadn't enjoyed his university placement working alongside psychology researchers over the past year doing different bits and pieces. He actually had but he was more than looking forward to the summer, spending time with his friends and family and just being excited about his final year at university.

The air was wonderfully cool and that was definitely one of the great benefits of it being midsummer. The air was fresh, crisp and wonderfully nature-scented, that left the delight taste of summer, mint and ice cream on his tongue, but the temperature would never ever get too hot or cold in the evening.

Something that was a massive benefit to living in the south of England. Sometimes it could be so hot people might as well be in places like Greece, but other times it could be so cold and bitter and awful that Josh might as well have lived in the artic.

Yet it was home and he always loved it, and he definitely couldn't imagine that living anywhere else would be any better for him.

The sound of the gentle evening breeze blowing through the trees making the branches gently tickle each other made Josh relax, and the ever-so-distant sound of cars making their way away from the university as everyone went home for the weekend, just made Josh feel more and more relaxed.

Something he was definitely going to need

tonight.

As much as he had loved his placement with his supervisor Graham and his supervisor's PhD student Matt. He couldn't deny that he wasn't excited about seeing Matt tonight and maybe, just maybe finally asking him out.

Josh had always been gay since he was a kid not that anyone really believed him. His friends hadn't shown that much interest in him since he came out, his parents just thought he was going through a strange phase and everyone else... Josh didn't actually know. Especially as he wasn't allowed to mention it in front of the wider family.

Josh couldn't really blame his parents too much. After all that they were probably of the generation that still seemed gays as strange curiosities that could be cured if given the right and proper guidance.

Josh looked as a little red car drove past him but it was the car of one of the lecturers going home. Not someone he would see tonight at the social.

But Josh was more than glad that his parents hadn't decided to give him any right and proper guidance about how to be straight. Which was great and everything, but Josh just wanted to be himself.

Granted Josh wasn't actually sure how to be himself anymore.

He had been closeted and forced to be straight for so long that he wasn't sure how to be gay, himself or what he actually wanted in relationships anymore.

When Josh had first come to university, he had

wanted to be gay, explore the scene and just live his own life a little away from the ever-watchful eye of his family. Which having a family that loves and wants to protect you is great, but definitely not when you want to be gay. Something they would (and do) most certainly frown upon.

Josh hadn't been gay, explored or ever really done much of anything to do with his sexuality. A fact that most definitely irritated and annoyed him, but he could understand it.

Josh followed the little narrow path to the left as it went away from the large road and through a little patch of woodland towards the bar the university social was at tonight.

The temperature dropped a few degrees and Josh just loved the great coolness that coated his skin. He just doubted that he was going to be his cool all night.

As Josh went through the woodland, he felt himself get more and more excited about seeing everyone tonight. It would be a great night filled with laughs, jokes and great conversations. Josh wasn't sure how many people were going to be there but there would be Graham, Matt and basically everyone who Graham monitors or tutors at the university.

Josh just smiled. When he first started his placement he never would have imagined that Graham tutored so many students but he really did. And Josh was more than pleased to meet up with so many other people.

But it was a shame that some of them wouldn't

be coming tonight. Like Josh's best friend Beth. Josh wasn't exactly clear where she was but all she had said on the phone earlier was it involved planes, jumping and men.

Josh was more than interested after the mention of men but then Beth had quickly cut the call and the strange sound of a damaged engine came from through the phone call, so Josh was certainly going to have to talk to her later on about that.

She really was something special. Crazy, concerning but very special.

Josh saw the end of the woodland as the path verged to the right and his entire stomach filled with butterflies.

He was almost at the university social and Matt was going to be there. The amazingly hot sexy and beautiful man that had kept him going throughout his placement, and actually been so nice to him.

Josh forced his stomach to relax. He had wanted to ask Matt out for months and he might finally be able to do it tonight and finally have a boyfriend.

His first ever one.

And that was something that excited Josh more than he wanted to admit.

CHAPTER 2
17th June 2022
Canterbury, England

Matt Daley sat on a very uncomfortable, hard wooden bench inside the *Woodlands Bar* at his university next to his best friend Tilly and girlfriend Alice as he waited for everyone to arrive for the social. It certainly was not one of his most favourite of places because of how awful the benches were, but it was what his PhD supervisor had wanted.

And Matt had decided a few hours of sitting on an uncomfortable bench would be worth it.

The entire bar was a strange combination of modern wood with its smooth wooden walls, long wooden benches and tables. And definitely ugly posters with so-called amazing accents of rock music and heavy metal.

Matt just couldn't believe how some people thought that his place actually worked, but that was life, and he was just focusing on seeing his friends,

Graham and hopefully a few other people.

The entire bar smelt… interesting with its hints of apples, pineapples and oranges from all the alcohol and cocktails that the bar specialised in (but even that was an overstatement), yet the bar also had a more subtle undertone of sweat that Matt seriously wasn't keen on.

But as he looked at his best friend in the entire world, Matt really didn't care he was just glad to be here and ready to celebrate the end of the academic year with his friends and other people Graham tutored.

Tilly was sat to his left looking up music on her phone and texting a random guy she was talking to. Matt had wanted her to invite him (more of his own his interest than Tilly's) but she was apparently dead set on making the random guy want to see her.

Matt didn't understand her frustration at the guy and all his random guy needed to do was see Tilly in her stunning little black dress (which was definitely overdressing for a university social) to see how amazing she was.

Matt felt two soft lips kiss his cheek and he wanted to pull away but he smiled and looked at his great-looking girlfriend Alice.

They had been together for over a year after meeting at last year's end-of-year social (which was the very uncool name of this social) and they had laughed, talked and been together for ages.

Alice was a great girl and she definitely looked

great in her tight jeans, white blouse and black shoes (again very overdressed for a university social) but Matt couldn't deny he was starting to get a little... unsettled in the relationship.

Well no that wasn't strictly true. Matt had to admit Alice was flat out amazing, he loved her and when they were alone she was just the best girlfriend ever, but this year had been tough.

Alice had actually asked him a few times why he had been downed, distracted or just not focusing on her at times through the year. Matt hadn't wanted to admit it to her because he did genuinely love her but ever since Josh had started working with Graham he did feel drawn to him at times.

It was even stranger because Josh was literally nothing special. He wasn't at all like the other guys Matt had dated in the past like the captain of the school's football team back in secondary school, or the most popular guy in his football team outside of school or even the outrageously fit guy he dated when he first started university ages ago.

Josh was just a really nice guy and as much as Matt just wanted to forget about him forever and just focus on Alice, he really couldn't sometimes.

And Matt was actually starting to feel a bit sad or something (he really couldn't name the emotion) that Josh wasn't going to be working with him next year. Sure Josh was focusing on doing his dissertation with Graham next year, but he wouldn't be working with Matt anymore.

And Matt couldn't deny that Josh had been acting "strange" for weeks. He wasn't being creepy or scary strange, but he was just being so nice, wonderful and kind that Matt couldn't understand why Josh was acting differently towards him.

Matt felt Alice wrap her wonderfully soft arms around him and she started kissing him again. Matt kissed her back and it was nice.

But that was it. It wasn't magical, amazing or anything he would ever write home about.

It was just nice.

A figure moved about at the corner of Matt's vision and he looked at who was walking through the massive open doors of the bar and he just smiled as he watched Josh's little eyes scan the room, find him and smile.

Josh was so beautiful that Matt almost wished he didn't have a girlfriend. But he did and he seriously liked Alice more than he ever wanted to admit.

CHAPTER 3
17th June 2022
Canterbury, England

It took everything Josh had not to fall to his knees the moment he saw Matt. Matt looked so outrageously sexy as he sat there on the wooden bench with two women next to him (Josh only recognised Tilly).

Josh seriously loved Matt's small handsome face with its slight beard, longish poufy dirty blond hair that Josh just seriously wanted to run his fingers through as he kissed Matt's soft wonderful lips.

Matt was just sheer perfection and even though Josh normally hated men in checkered trousers (because come on, they are a crime against humanity and fashion) Josh just didn't care and Matt actually pulled them off wonderfully. And Josh seriously had to focus when he noticed that Matt had a button or two of his white shirt undone revealing his small fit chest.

Granted it was covered in chest hair which was something that normally turned off Josh, but Josh just couldn't believe how amazing and sexy Matt looked tonight. This was going to be a sensational night and Josh was just looking forward to talking, seeing and hopefully asking Matt out.

It took a moment for Josh to realise he was still standing up and Matt was smiling at him. He went over said hello to Matt and the two girls and couldn't believe how awfully uncomfortable the benches were. If Josh had had some fat or muscle on his butt then he probably wouldn't have felt a thing, but he was mostly bone. These benches were very uncomfortable.

Josh was about to start talking to Matt before the two girls could deny him that privilege, but the sounds of more happy hellos beat him to it.

Josh didn't bother to get up as three more women all in different summer dresses and flat walking shoes (definitely a good choice for eating and drinking in here) all came in, shook his hand and said hello.

Josh knew them from other socials and they were all amazing, full of laughs and the night was definitely going to be a fun one. Yet the only major problem was that he had no idea what each of them were called.

Two arms wrapped round him in a quick hug as a very tall woman in a long pink summer dress sat down next to him. Josh had no clue what this woman was called but given how on the very first social the two of them had ended up talking about left-wing politics. Josh just called her Left-Wing Girl.

Then another woman wearing a long black dress with dyed red hair said hello to Josh as he sat down on the other side. Again Josh had no clue what her name was so Josh just called her Vegan-Girl but she was a very proud and firm vegan. Which Josh could completely understand he had his own vegan rules, like tonight because he was out and away from home he would be a vegan.

It was better than nothing. And him and Vegan-Girl would probably end up talking about veganism later on anyway, but all Josh really wanted to talk about and to was wonderfully beautifully Matt.

Josh was again just about to try to talk to Matt who was literally just a metre away from him on the opposite side of the table when a very tall man wearing a black suit, shoes and a straw hat walked in.

Josh had no clue why Graham was wearing a straw hat but he supposed he didn't need to know. Everyone said their hellos, heys and other pointless things to each other as they all got settled.

There was little doubt that Graham would be over to talk to Josh at some point, but Josh had no problem with that. He really liked Graham and it was going to be great working with him some more next year.

It was just a shame he wasn't going to be working with Matt too, that was definitely the biggest problem with next year.

It marked the end of working with stunning Matt.

"What do you want to drink?" Graham asked everyone as he gestured he was going to the bar and was buying the first round.

Well. Josh wasn't entirely sure that was true because he was still rather surprised that the university allowed Graham to spend his grant money on things like food, drinks and activities for socials. So either the university or Graham was actually paying for it, either way that hardly mattered.

"Diet coke please," Josh said as everyone told Graham their own orders.

Josh smiled as he watched the strange looks he was getting from other people.

"I'm driving," Josh said.

"I'm driving too but I still want to have some fun," Left-Wing Girl said.

Josh didn't really want to start getting into how he could have plenty of fun without drinking and alcohol and whatever these drinking university people thought they needed. But he just smiled.

"And I don't like the taste or the effects," Josh said.

Everyone nodded and went back to their conversations and Josh started talking to Left-Wing Girl about her year, how her Masters was going and if there was anything else interesting going on.

It turned out there was, but as much as Josh

loved listening to it all. Including how her research was going, how her boyfriend was (who Josh admitted was fairly hot) and her plans for the future. Josh just couldn't stop watching Matt out of the corner of his eye.

Josh loved seeing his smile, laugh and stare rather strangely into the large brown eyes of the mystery woman sitting next to him.

Until now Josh hadn't given her much thought because she was surely just something to do with Graham and had absolutely no interest in Matt whatsoever.

Then their mouths got closer and Josh felt his stomach tighten into a painful knot.

That was Matt's girlfriend.

Matt, the stunningly beautiful man that was so nice, kind and wonderful, wasn't gay in the slightest.

Josh just wanted the ground to swollen him up and never spit him back out.

CHAPTER 4
17th June 2022
Canterbury, England

Of course he had a girlfriend.

Josh just flat out couldn't believe what was happening. This was completely ridiculous. He had been so sure that Matt, this amazing hot sexy man who Josh had seen look so perfect with his gorgeous smile, painted nails and gay mannerisms was actually straight.

This was just outrageous.

Josh looked at Matt and his girlfriend kiss more and more and laugh and smile to themselves and he just felt so sick. It was like he had been stabbed in the stomach and thrown on the ground. This wasn't how his perfect magical night was meant to go, it was meant to be wonderful, relaxing and filled with happiness.

Something that clearly wasn't happening now.

As much as Josh wanted to go home, crawl into

his bed and never come out again. He knew that he had to at least try to be happy, stick around and maybe things would turn out differently. Like Matt and his girlfriend could have a massive fight, Matt could be upset and need a caring hand to help him.

Of course Josh wasn't that sort of person, but if it happened he was hardly going to past over the opportunity. He was gay, not straight.

"Are you listening to me?" Left-Wing Girl asked.

Josh realised that she had been talking to him about her family and he had been pretending to listen when all he really wanted to do was watch Matt.

But as the silly happy couple laughed, smiled and talked with each other, all Josh could bring himself to do was nod at Left-Wing Girl as she kept talking about herself again.

Out of everything that could have happened tonight Josh seriously hadn't been expecting that whatsoever. Sure he had only ever guessed that Matt was gay, but he supposed that some straight men might act a little "camp" and wear a little nail polish from time to time.

This just sucked.

Josh partly wished that straight people were actually banned from acting gay, wearing nail polish and just doing anything that might mislead him. But he wasn't that sure, he had seriously wanted Matt to be gay.

He just wanted to be with this stunningly beautiful man.

"I'm grabbing a drink. You want something?" Left-Wing Girl asked.

"No thanks," Josh said.

The last thing he wanted was for other people to spend their hard earned cash on him.

"Josh," Matt said.

Josh felt a wave of pleasure wash over him as Matt smiled from across the table. There was just something in how Matt said his name that made him get excited, happy and feeling as light as a feather.

Josh smiled at Matt, and seriously tried not to frown or pull a funny face at his girlfriend.

Matt and Josh quickly exchanged their *heys* and *how are yous*, but Josh was more than happy to lie through his teeth. He felt awful, his night was ruined and he seriously he didn't like Matt's girlfriend who was sitting there so... Josh wasn't sure. He just didn't like her.

"You haven't met Alice before have you?"

Josh seriously forced himself not to smile. Of course how the hell could he have met her? If he had then he could have spared himself months upon months of feelings and emotional heartache over pining for a man that he could never be with.

But Josh decided he had to play nice and he would never be rude, horrible or unkind to Matt. Matt was far too perfect for that. Well maybe the only crime was he had acted too gay in the past for a straight person and sent Josh the wrong signals.

Besides from that Matt was perfect.

"No I haven't," Josh said extending his hand to Alice.

She smiled and shook it. Josh shook it hard. It was probably a little painful for her but at this point Josh was seriously passed the point of caring.

Josh tried (and failed) not to smile as Alice took her hand away and shook it, almost as if she was trying to force the blood back into it.

"How long have you two been together?" Josh asked.

Matt smiled and looked around and it was almost looked like he was checking to see if Graham wasn't anywhere nearby. Thankfully for Matt he wasn't, Graham was talking to some of the other students on the opposite end of the table.

"I'll get us drinks," Alice said.

Josh hated the sound of her voice, but maybe he was just being petty. Then Alice kissed Matt again and went over to the bar.

"Graham doesn't know," Matt said.

Josh had absolutely no clue how Graham couldn't know. Josh had only been here half an hour and had been basically in love with Matt for months and he was only just finding out about it.

How the hell Graham didn't know with him and Matt working side by side every day was beyond Josh.

"How?" Josh asked.

Matt smiled. Josh flat out loved it when Matt smiled. It was so cute.

"I don't know. He's sort of clueless about it,"

Josh wasn't going to deny that.

"How long have you two been together?" Josh asked again.

Matt frowned sort of and smiled sort of.

"About a year. We met this time last time,"

Now that actually wasn't as bad as what Josh feared. He supposed he could live with that, at least it wasn't a case of a month or two or three that would make Josh fear for the rest of his life that *if only* he had asked Matt out months earlier.

At least he didn't have that to bear.

"These socials can be amazing," Matt said.

Bastard.

Josh so badly wanted to come up with some sort of come back about how Matt and Alice had ruined this social and now Josh was going to die sad and alone.

"Well no offense. I thought you were gay," Josh said.

He had no clue where that came from but it was true, and it was only now that Josh was starting to understand how annoyed he actually was. After everything that had happened to him with his friends, family and the bullying over the years, Josh finally thought he had found a great guy that could make him happy.

Nope.

That wasn't going to happen and it was clear as day as Josh was meant to suffer in silence and never ever be happy.

And that made Josh just want to cry.

CHAPTER 5
17th June 2022
Canterbury, England

Matt was absolutely shocked that Josh would even think or say something like that. Sure he was bisexual and he loved guys and everything that went along with all that side of himself, but he wasn't gay.

And why the hell would Josh say something like that in public and like he did. He almost sounded pissed or really annoyed.

Matt could feel his face bend in confusion and slight shock at the comment, but he couldn't deny that he wasn't mad about it. And he just looked at Josh for a moment and… he really did look good tonight.

Matt really liked Josh's white shirt that highlighted his slim body, his tight blue jeans and his trainers that was actually okay for this awful bar. Even from here Matt could smell Josh's wonderfully earthy spicy aftershave that made Matt's heart skip a beat.

But it was still so strange that Josh would say that. Sure Matt had worn a bit of nail polish months ago during one of their meetings but he hadn't thought that that screamed he was gay or only into men.

And more importantly he hadn't known anyone to actually focus or realise that little detail. The only people who had realised that sort of detail were his friends, family and… gay men.

Matt was even more shocked now as he quickly realised that Josh was actually gay. He had had some suspicions and questions because of some of the things Josh had said, but now he had confirmed it was great.

Matt didn't know why he was so pleased but he actually felt so much lighter, happier and like he really, really wanted to talk with Josh even more.

The sounds of other people talking, laughing and failing badly to sing the songs the bar was playing reminded Matt that he wasn't alone, and that sooner or later his wonderful girlfriend would come back.

And what if Josh liked him and Alice found out? Would she be mad, angry or something? Would she attack or moan at Josh?

Matt didn't want that so maybe it would be best if he just finished up the conversation quickly and went away from wonderful Josh before the two could meet properly.

"No," Matt said. "But I go both ways,"

It was all Matt could think to say, he didn't want

to say he was outright bisexual because he wasn't sure if he strictly identified as that in the strictest sense. He just liked who he liked regardless of whether it was a man or woman. And lying to Josh just felt criminal.

"Okay," Josh said.

Matt couldn't help but feel a little guilty. It wasn't like Josh was sad or anything but Matt could "sense" or at least feel like there was more to that story that Matt seriously wanted to explore.

"Hi guys," Graham said as he sat next to Matt and Josh just waved at him.

As Graham started talking to Josh about life stuff, Matt just realised that he actually didn't want Graham there or anyone else in the bar. He just wanted to talk with Josh to at least get to know him better.

Of course he would never do anything with Josh because Matt was fairly sure he wasn't interested in Josh in the slightest, and he would never mistreat or cheat on Alice. She was a good girlfriend and very nice and that meant something to Matt.

A few minutes later as Matt watched Alice in her very nice dress get some drinks and was about to start walking back over before she started talking to the barman again, he felt a hand tap his arm.

Matt looked back at Graham and smiled as his supervisor clearly wanted to ask a question or something.

"Where do stand on having children?" Graham asked.

Matt didn't know what the hell he had missed since he was staring at beautiful Alice, but he had clearly missed something.

"What?" Matt asked.

"Well Josh here was asking about me having kids. I don't as you know because I don't mind the idea of having them but I don't want to add to the human population as you know. But we were wondering about you?"

Matt couldn't help but feel harsh or bad for his real answer, but considering how they were all friends were and maybe his true answer would horrify and hopefully make Josh like him less. He decided he had to tell it.

"I don't want kids," Matt said. "I can't abide them and I don't have the patients for them. If a student isn't understanding statistics I can have all the patience in the world, but if a kid's doing something silly. I don't have the patience,"

Matt had always hated looking after his sister's kids for a few hours because… they were just awful. Well they weren't badly behaved, they were just children that liked playing with things, knocking things over and all the other things that other people thought were adorable. Matt just didn't like that.

He was almost concerned that Josh was going to be mad or something, but he just sat there smiling like he understood or at least respected Matt's opinion.

And he didn't know exactly why but he liked that feeling. It had been ages since he had actually said his true opinion on having children and no one had judged him.

Matt refused to talk about the topic with his family because with him having so many brothers and sisters it felt weird not adding to the family, and that was how everyone saw it too.

And he was hardly going to talk about it with Alice with them only dating for a year, but even when he had mentioned it in passing she hadn't been impressed. So for someone (especially someone Matt didn't know too well) to respect him, it felt strange.

But a good type of strange.

"Nice," Josh said.

"What about you?" Graham asked.

Matt leant closer a little and was a bit surprised when Josh just looked at him, like his answer was directed at him personally.

"I don't know really. I'm not too fussed and I quite like the idea of giving back the kids to the parents at the end of the day. I like playing with them but not forever,"

Matt definitely agreed with that.

"But if I ever found the right person and they wanted kids I think I would like them but it's all about finding the right person," Josh said smiling.

As Graham talked on, Matt felt a little warm and cold inside at the same time. He wasn't sure how to take it, was Josh talking to him?

Was he Josh's right man?

He didn't know and as much as he wanted to

find out and get to know Josh a little better. Alice called him out.

And Matt had to go and leave his great-looking man behind.

CHAPTER 6
17th June 2022
Canterbury, England

Laughter, singing and chatting filled up the rest of the amazing night for Matt as he talked with everyone else at the wonderful social. He had drunk a good amount but he wasn't tipsy or drunk in the slightest.

The smell of apples, pineapples and sugar syrups filled the air as the bar kept making more and more cocktails for the various groups of people sprinkled throughout the bar. That left the amazing taste of porn star martinis form on his tongue. They had to be his favourite.

It was about nine o'clock and surprisingly enough the bar was rather empty except for a few other groups of people. Granted it was the last day of the university year so tons of people had already gone home but Matt was still really glad to be here with Tilly, Alice and the others.

Graham had already gone home because he needed to cycle and the last time he (and Matt included) wanted was for him to cycling in the dark and get involved in a crash. Matt seriously didn't want that.

Alice had her long skinny legs across Matt's lags and Tilly was telling them about her random guy and how they had promised to meet up tomorrow.

Matt was so glad to hear that, it was about time Tilly actually got out into the world and experienced the wonderful pleasures that men could give a person.

And Matt carefully ran his fingers up Alice's legs which she didn't mind, and he just couldn't stop flicking glances over to Josh who was talking, smiling and engaging with everyone.

But him.

Matt knew it was so silly to be curious or jealous that other people got the chance to talk to Josh except him. It wasn't even like Josh was avoiding him, it was more like the other way.

Matt just knew that he couldn't spend all night talking to Josh because surely Josh wanted to talk to other people, and he certainly couldn't leave Alice and Tilly all night without him.

That would just be cruel.

And having Alice upset or suspicious was definitely the last thing he wanted. Alice knew he was bisexual and had been with men for the two relationships before her, and even though he kept saying she was find with it whenever Matt went out with his gay friends. He could always tell that she was nervous about it all.

The last thing Matt wanted was to accidentally confirm her suspicions.

And it wasn't like Matt even liked Josh really. Sure he was cute, amazing and a wonderful man but he wasn't relationship material and he probably wasn't even interested in Matt in the first place.

All that stuff about finding the right man to have kids with and all that was probably just Matt reading too much into things. That had to be the answer, it just had to be.

"Bye everyone!" Josh said loudly.

As everyone waved, said goodbyes and said how great it was to see Josh (and it honestly was), Matt just felt a little sad that he was now stuck here without him.

Well he was stuck here with his best friend and Alice which wasn't a bad thing in itself, but he really wished Josh could stay a little longer.

Then Matt noticed Josh was looking specifically at him so Matt gave him a schoolboy smile and waved. He really hoped that Alice didn't see that smile, but he hadn't meant it.

And as he watched Josh go, he couldn't take his eyes away from him until he was gone completely out of sight.

But he certainly wasn't out of mind.

"He's a great guy," Tilly said.

Matt nodded.

"Still wondering what Beth was up to today," Tilly said.

Matt forced his mind to get back into gear and focus so he run his fingers gently up and down Alice's good-looking legs a few more times.

"He's probably just making it up. Let's talk about me," Alice said.

Matt wanted to protest and go back to talking about Beth and Josh, but he had learnt a long time ago that some fights weren't worth the effort, and this was one of them.

About an hour later the rest of the university people had left from the social and Matt sat there with Alice sleeping on his shoulder and Tilly was finishing up a large glass of whiskey (Matt was so glad she was staying at his house tonight) and he really wished that Josh was still here, just to talk.

"What you thinking about?" Tilly asked.

Matt just smiled. He wasn't going to tell her not with Alice being such good friends with her. Alice had probably told Tilly about her bisexual concerns so he definitely wasn't going to tell her.

"Nothing much. Had fun tonight?" Matt asked.

Tilly shook her head and smiled. "You are allowed to think about Josh,"

Matt looked at the floor slightly.

"I know you like him as a friend. You've always mentioned how great of a person he is and how nice he is to you. Why don't you just ask him out as a friend? Bring him out on one of our night outs,"

"No," Matt said firmly

He honestly hadn't meant to say it as loud as he did, but Matt wasn't going to let any poor soul come out with them and Tilly on a drinking night out. That was dangerous, lethal and just something Matt didn't want to put Josh through. And he had already mentioned that he didn't like alcohol.

"Just," Tilly said slowly. "Just don't be scared to have a friend because of what *she* might think,"

Matt looked at good-looking Alice as she slept. She was a very nice and great girlfriend that honestly loved him, and he her. But he did wish she would let him have more gay friends he was never going to cheat on her.

Wasn't his word enough?

"You know deary," Tilly said resting her chin on his shoulder. "Text Josh or something, or I'll go down the corner shop when we get back to yours and I'll buy three bottles of vodka,"

Matt smiled because she wasn't joking. Tilly never ever joked about alcohol and drinking and buying bottles. She had done it before and Matt's head still hurt from all the alcohol so he would rather skip that torture.

And the last thing he wanted was to get completely drunk and possibly say something about a guy to Alice.

Matt just playfully hit Tilly on the head and took out his phone.

He needed to send a quick text.

Matt just hoped it wouldn't do more harm than good.

PART TWO: NURSING A BROKEN HEART

BREAKING, NURSING, REPAIRING A BROKEN HEART

CHAPTER 7
18th June 2022
Rochester, England

It might have been three o'clock in the afternoon the day after that awful university social but Josh still couldn't bring himself to do much anything. It was silly, pathetic and stupid but Josh seriously couldn't be bothered to get out of his small single bed that would forever be destined to be cold and lonely with him being the only person in it.

Small shivers of cold distant sunlight pierced through Josh's long blue curtains and it dimly illuminated his large bedroom with its wardrobe, wooden desk and glass cabinets filled with bits and pieces struggling to become lit in the little light he allowed in the room.

As Josh's mum had put it so perfectly earlier when she gave to lovingly check on him, the entire room gave off such intense dark apocalyptic gloomy vibes that matched Josh's mood perfectly.

It wasn't even like Josh was too upset about Matt having a girlfriend. She seemed perfectly nice, wonderful and it was clear that she truly loved Matt. The problem was something that Josh just couldn't put his finger on.

Not that he actually wanted to lift a finger or anything to try and find out what the problem was. He was more than "happy" wrapped up in his thick bedsheets and not eating or drinking for the day. It was a shame that his mum and dad had to go out to see his grandparents because there was a slight emergency, but Josh couldn't deny that he did just want one day of being mopey and pathetic.

A few moments later, Josh heard the distinct sound of someone knocking on the front door all the way downstairs, and as much as Josh wanted to answer it. He was quickly starting to realise he was so depressed that even flicking the sheets off him seemed like an impossible feat.

Then Josh heard the distant sound of the door's lock turning and the door opening. Then whoever this weird stranger was, they were at least kind enough to lock the door and slowly make their way upstairs.

In normal situations Josh might have panicked, grabbed a pair of scissors from his desk and try to defend himself. But if he couldn't have Matt and he was doomed to die alone then he might as well speed up the process.

And he wasn't entirely sure if he was joking or

not. Even if this person wasn't a strange robber, Josh was definitely going to force himself up in a moment and start slowly returning to the land of the living and the unheartbroken (well that was a bit more ambitious but it was a good idea at the very least).

The sound of footsteps stopped outside Josh's large white bedroom door and then the handle slowly turned and someone tried to get in.

They couldn't.

Josh looked at the very bottom of the bedroom door and smiled when he saw a pair of boxers were right in front of the door stopping anyone from getting in. After his mum visited earlier Josh really hadn't wanted any more visitors so putting clothes there was always a good idea.

"Josh for god sake open the door," Beth said.

Josh couldn't believe that his best friend in the entire world was actually here. He had no idea why she was here, how she knew he was upset or something but he was more than glad she was here.

"Joshua," Beth said.

Josh laughed and really forced himself to throw back the bedsheets and since standing and walking was far too much effort. He simply crawled over to the bedroom door, removed the pair of boxers and simply crawled back into bed.

It didn't take long for Beth to come through the door and Josh had to admit she looked wonderful today. He didn't know what he would call her little outfit but her denim shorts, vest top and trainers certainly gave her the girl-next-door look that plenty of men seemed to love.

"This place stinks!" Beth shouted as she went over to the windows and opened them.

"Hi Beth," Josh said forcefully.

He didn't even want to speak but if Beth was here, Josh seriously knew that wasn't an option anytime soon.

"Darling," Beth said. "Care to tell me why I get a very upset phone call from my best friend, his mother and his father all in the space of an hour,"

Josh's eyes widened. He had absolutely no clue he had called her last night, but after leaving the bar the entire night was a bit hazy. Josh knew that he drove home, was very upset and talked to his parents about their wish about him not dating Matt was going to be true.

The bastards.

Yet Josh had no idea when he had phoned Beth, so he picked up his phone and checked it.

"Oh god," Josh said.

It seemed that the world really, really hated Josh for some reason. He wasn't impressed that there was a late night message from Matt on his phone.

In an ideal world, the message might be something along the lines of *hi Josh, you were so beautiful last night that I decided to breakup with Alice and be with you.*

Josh just laughed at that silly idea. He really wasn't that sort of person and he would never ever want Matt to break off a good thing for Alice just for an idiot like him. But he couldn't deny how badly he wanted Matt to at least send him something suggestive or just an offer to be friends.

"What?" Beth asked as she sat down on Josh's bed.

Josh passed Beth his phone. "Read that text for me. It's too painful to do it myself,"

Josh couldn't believe how pathetic that sounded and he had to get up in a moment, he couldn't be like this all day and night.

"All it says darling is, *Hey, just wanted to thank you for coming earlier. It was very nice to see you. Have a lovely summer*," Beth said. "Seems harmless,"

Josh rolled his eyes. That was the point. Matt was just such a nice wonderful guy who was sweet, thoughtful and so, so caring that Josh would love to be with someone like him.

Beth stood up and folded her arms. "Darling. Your parents phoned me earlier because they wouldn't be back until tomorrow and they didn't want you being alone. I have my suitcases outside. You get up, help me move in for the night and then we can get you back to normal,"

As Josh felt Beth pull his arm and forced him to get up and go downstairs he seriously loved her determination.

But he seriously doubted that anything except a miracle could make him feel better and go back to normal.

CHAPTER 8
18th June 2022
Rochester, England

Normally when people decide to bring a suitcase or two to their friend's house, it is literally one or two suitcases and that is it. Josh had absolutely no clue where Beth had gone but clearly it was something that needed a hell of a lot of baggage and utter crap.

As Josh sat under a large deadly black blanket to match his mood on his equally large and dark sofa, he watched Beth as she finished looking through all her rubbish and suitcases and she looked as if she was actually trying to organise the mess in front of her.

If Josh wasn't outright gay with thankfully no hope of ever being straight, he probably would have run like hell out of his own living room at the sight of all the stuff. Josh had little idea how much make-up, condoms and other things that Beth packed for her travels.

And it was clear as day that one of her perfume

bottles had broken on the way home. The entire living room smelt of lilacs, violets and lavender to create a strangely wonderful aroma.

Yet it still didn't smell anywhere near as great as Matt.

"Where did you go?" Josh asked.

"I went on an adventure camp for two days. It was rather wonderful really it was filled with mud, hot sweaty men and plenty of survival training," Beth said.

Josh nodded. In a past life he would have loved that, a few years ago before he went to university he had been a part of a youth organisation that was in all that, but then the bullying, abuse and even some beatings started all because he was gay. So that was firmly in the past and Josh was never going to do anything like that again.

"It still hurts, doesn't it?" Beth asked, as she came over with two large mugs of velvety hot chocolate with whipped cream and marshmallows and sat on the sofa with him.

Josh didn't dare say anything. He had burdened Beth with all this the last time and she hadn't been too great. It's one thing to know that gays can and sometimes do get beaten up, but it was apparently quite another to see your best friend since infant school beaten and blackened.

"What's really bothering you?" Beth asked, playfully kicking Josh's feet.

Josh smiled at the bad attempt to make him

laugh but he just shrugged.

"I know how much you liked Matt. And I wasn't even sure he was still with Alice," Beth said.

Josh planted his face in his hands. His own best friend knew that Matt was in a relationship and she didn't even tell him. Why would she do that? If she had she could have saved Josh all this pain and suffering and annoyance.

"I was sure they would have broken up by now," Beth said smiling.

"You're lying," Josh said.

Beth smiled and nodded.

Josh shook his head and took a large wonderful mouthful of the creamy sweet hot chocolate. This was probably what him and Matt would have done on their first date as they laughed, talked and just got to know each other more and more.

"Come on," Beth said as she pointed towards the massive TV in front of them. "What you want to watch? Gay romance?"

Josh put his drink on the little coffee table in front of them and just snuggled into the sofa and blankets. A romance was the very last thing he ever wanted to watch again.

Beth carefully moved over and wrapped her thin arms around him.

"You'll survive this. You always do," Beth said.

Josh forced himself away from her and felt so angry. He didn't want to survive anymore. He wanted to start living.

"I don't want to survive! I want to love, have relationships and be me! I don't want other fucking idiots telling me what I can and can't do. I want to know what love is. I want to…"

Josh hadn't noticed that Beth had gotten up from the sofa and was hugging him tight.

"I know you do," Beth said. "I know you thought this was your shot to be gay, happy and have a relationship,"

Josh just buried his face into his neck, and that was the real problem it wasn't that Matt actually had a girlfriend. It was that after years of abuse, bullying and denying himself, Josh just wanted, needed to have a shot at being himself.

And he really thought that Matt was the one amazing wonderful guy that was going to help him be himself.

"You know darling," Beth said. "Do you remember my philosophy about men?"

"If he doesn't have an 8-inch dick then he's no good in bed," Josh said.

Beth playfully hit him round the head. Josh just laughed because it was definitely one of her rules about men, a rule that she almost never stood by, but clearly there were more rules than Josh realised.

"Honesty," Beth said.

Josh shook his head. "How can I be honest with him? What would I say. *Hi Matt, I know you have a girlfriend but I really like you and want you to bang me?*"

"Well," Beth said. "Obviously not quite like that

but I know you want to just send him a message that would make you feel better. And tomorrow we can start anew as the old folk say,"

Josh wasn't sure about it. He didn't know what he would ever send Matt after last night, but he supposed he could at least apologise for accusing him of being gay.

Maybe that was a start.

A start that could lead to more?

CHAPTER 9
18th June 2022
Canterbury, England

It might have been a few minutes to midnight but Matt had honestly loved spending time with great-looking Alice. They had had a good dinner out on Canterbury High Street at a wonderful Italian place, they had laughed and had a lot of adult fun.

But as Matt laid in his large double bed with Alice peacefully sleeping next to him with her nice-looking head resting on his chest, Matt was just a bit unsettled.

Tonight had been great fun and it was very nice to be spending it with Alice a woman that honestly loved him. But everything was just nice about it all, Alice was a very nice woman, the sex was very nice and something about their relationship was just nice.

There was nothing amazing, outrageously sexy or any strong burning feelings between it.

Matt felt horrible to be feeling like this after

everything Alice had done for him, but he just wasn't sure if this was what he wanted for his life. A relationship where everything was just okay and nice.

Tilly had once mentioned about having sex with a man was rather magical, passionate and sheer pleasure, and Matt completely agreed. He had always preferred gay sex to straight sex, there was just more passion, love and something more primal about it all.

Matt shook that idea away as Alice started snoring a little. She was cute when she snored and she was cute a lot of the time, but Matt couldn't help but feel like he wanted more, a lot more.

Matt's phone buzzed and Matt just ignored it. He was already unsettled enough so looking at his phone and getting all that blue light wouldn't help him anymore.

Laying on the floor next to Matt's bed, Tilly started snoring louder and louder, and he was really glad that she hadn't been in the room when him and Alice were having fun so Matt just smiled. He had actually forgotten how much she snored when she was drunk. Thankfully Tilly wasn't a bad drunk or anything like that, but she was still cruel for making Matt text Josh, that perfectly cute adorable boy.

Another intense snor made Matt roll his eyes and check his phone.

He had no clue why Josh would be texting him this late at night. He had heard from a friend of a friend that Beth was staying with him tonight but surely both of them would be far, far too tired to be up this late?

Matt swiped his phone and read the message and he honestly felt sorry for Josh.

"And I just wanted to say I'm really sorry for saying you were gay. Really sorry. It won't happen again. Have a great summer. See you around"

Matt honestly didn't know what it was about the message but he just wanted to hug Josh and tell him he was okay. Josh was clearly stressed or something and was having some kind of troubles.

Matt really wanted to just reach out, call him and offer some kind of support. He must have felt bad about it, but Matt couldn't understand why?

He hadn't been rude or offended when Josh had called him that. He was actually slightly happy that Josh did, but there just had to be something else. Something that he wasn't seeing.

"Why that boy texting you this late?" Alice slowly asked.

Matt focused back on his phone and realised that Alice was reading it all, and she hardly looked happy.

"Tell him to go away and get a life. You're mine. Stop texting him too," Alice said as she went back to sleep.

Matt turned his screen brightness to the lowest setting and just looked at the message for a moment. There had to be more to the message, Josh had something on his mind and Matt couldn't bear the idea of Josh being in emotional pain.

The last thing Matt was going to do was what

Alice suggested, but he was going to play it cool and just hope beyond hope that Josh could be okay at some point.

So he texted back quick: *No worries. It's fine. Have a lovely summer, relax and see you next year.*

It was a lame text Matt was certain of that, but it was now past midnight, he was tired and he wanted Josh to be okay. But maybe he needed to talk to someone who was a bit more neutral than him and Alice.

Maybe he needed to talk to Tilly.

Alone.

CHAPTER 10
19th June 2022
Canterbury, England

The wonderful smells of fried eggs, bacon and hash browns filled the air as Matt and Tilly went a small café located in one of the little side streets to Canterbury High Street.

Matt had always loved its little cosy booths, red leather chairs and wonderful atmosphere that made it perfect for different students to get together and carefully plot their coursework and exams without other people overhearing.

Matt was more impressed with Tilly than he had been for a long time. He hadn't expected her to stay for two nights and she had had no almost slept since him and Alice went out for their evening fun, and she still looked amazing.

After two days of no sleeping, partying and being an amazing friend she still looked spectacular in her Demin shorts, white blouse and white high heels. It certainly wasn't a great look but somehow Tilly managed to pull it off perfectly.

"Why you want to talk without Alice?" Tilly asked as they both sat down in a little booth far away from the wait staff that were currently clearing up after the lunch crowd.

Matt was slightly surprised at the coolness of the red leather booths and he pulled two menus from the end of the booth and passed one over to Tilly.

"Have you ever been in love before?" Matt asked.

Tilly smiled. "You know how good of a friend I am with Alice, right?"

Matt's mouth dropped. He had completely forgotten with how fatigued he was and all the mysterious emotions that Josh's stressed message kicked up in him.

Tilly laughed. "Relax. I'm your friend first and Alice is... nice,"

Matt felt like such a fool. He really, really liked Alice but even his best friend wasn't sure about love or whatever he had been tricking himself into.

So Matt quickly told her about Josh's text last night.

"Well," Tilly said laughing. "It says like you need to talk to him. Get ask him what's bothering him and get him to open up,"

Matt shook his head. "I can't Alice would be furious about that. She doesn't want me to be talking to him or anything,"

Tilly folded her arms and Matt felt bad as he realised Tilly was refusing to look at him as her cold eyes looked up and down the menu.

"Tell me this Mathew," Tilly said. "Without us being too harsh, you do really think Josh had had that many chances to be gay in his little life?"

Matt smiled. That was probably the best point she had ever made, and Tilly used to be leader of the Debating Society so good points were sort of her special skill.

"No," Matt said.

"Do you fancy or do you like him romantically?" Tilly asked.

The question sort of caught Matt off-guard for some reason and he wasn't exactly sure what his true answer would be, but he just shook his head.

"I need words," Tilly said smiling.

"No I don't like him like that," Matt said.

He felt so strange as he said that like he was completely lying to himself and like he was the worse person ever, but he liked Alice. He really did and he would never want to hurt her.

"Okay then," Tilly said. "So you aren't attracted to him, you love Alice, so what's the harm in just talking to someone?"

Matt didn't want to answer. The last thing he wanted was for Alice to find out and accuse him of cheating on her with another man.

"Let me put in this way," Tilly said. "Did you ever listen to Josh talking a few socials back about his gay experience?"

Matt smiled. He had hung onto every word that came out of his beautiful mouth (not Alice beautiful of course), then Matt realised what Tilly was getting at.

"Oh," Matt said. "You think… he just wants a friend. A person to talk to,"

Tilly waved her hand over to a very young waitress that went to the university and she ordered herself a cup of tea, and Matt ordered himself a mug of coffee.

"Yes," Tilly said. "Just go out with Josh. Say it's not a date and just see what's bothering him. I seem to remember a very young bi Mathew struggling and needing to talk,"

Matt just frowned at Tilly at the seriousness of her tone, but she was right of course. Coming out as bi for him wasn't exactly perfectly easy. It was easy compared to other stories he had heard but there were still a few problems he had to hash out.

"I just don't want Alice to think I'm cheating on her,"

Tilly huffed. "Mathew for god sake. You have the right to have gay friends and if your girlfriend cannot handle that then surely she doesn't deserve you,"

Matt smiled as at least he finally knew what his best friend really thought about him and his girlfriend. And she did have a point maybe he should just reach out, make sure everyone was okay and maybe offer

Josh a helping hand.

He just hoped his act of kindness wouldn't come back to bite him.

BREAKING, NURSING, REPAIRING A BROKEN HEART

CHAPTER 11
19th June 2022
Canterbury, England

Of all the texts Josh had expected to receive today he never ever would have guessed beautiful, sexy Matt to text him and ask him out (but not a date). But the stranger thing was that Beth had also gotten a text from Tilly about them two and Alice going out.

Josh had laughed as he listened to Beth's protests about going out with Alice considering she was the one who had stolen Josh's happiness. But Josh had just told her to go, have fun and maybe she would meet a very nice boy out there in the real world.

Josh sat in a cold wooden booth at an Italian restaurant near the back. The view was rather good considering how many people were out tonight to watch some kind of football game and then drink into the early hours.

Josh and Matt certainly weren't going to be doing

that, but all the noise of the football game playing on the TV, people ordering drinks and food made Josh feel safe for some reason.

The whole feeling safe thing was probably just another echo of him not drinking and how straight sporty boys never liked it when gays and non-real-men went into their spaces. But that was the past and Josh just wanted to focus on the future.

A hopeful future with Matt but that was next to impossible.

"Hey," Matt said as he sat down opposite Josh.

Josh felt his heart pound in his chest, his stomach filled with butterflies and sweat started to pour down his back. Matt looked so amazing and hot in his tight white shirt, black jeans that left little to the imagination and his wonderful poufy hair.

He was sheer perfection.

Matt looked so much better than Josh did in his jeans, shirt and trainers. This had been a bad idea, a very bad idea.

Josh should have just stayed at home and been depressed. He shouldn't have bothered-

Matt touched his hand and pure chemistry, power and love flowed between them. Josh loved the feeling of Matt's rough fingers against his smooth hand.

"Are you okay?" Matt asked.

Josh honestly didn't know. He was in a restaurant with a perfect guy that he was in love with but could never be with, he was scared because of his past that he would be verbally abused in such a manly sporty place and he just felt... rubbish.

"Why did you want to do this tonight?" Josh asked.

Josh watched Matt for a moment and Josh was surprised to see that Matt also wasn't sure.

"I don't really know. You've been on my mind for ages and I just wanted to talk and... I don't know," Matt said.

Josh took two menus from the waiter as he walked round and Josh loved the amazing smell of golden crispy fried chicken in creamy mash potatoes that filled the air.

"Can I be honest with you?" Josh asked.

He didn't know how to just tell Matt that he liked him and everything, but considering he was always going to ask Matt out in the end. He didn't really see the harm in just telling him, and after all it wasn't like he had anything left to lose.

"Of course," Matt said. "Why did you text me in the dead of night?"

Josh smiled. "I really like you and I was going to ask you out properly today actually. So Friday was a bit of a surprise to me and you were really on my mind ever since, so I sent the text just to get you off my mind,"

Josh was really pleased that he felt so much lighter, happier and more relaxed. He honestly felt a hundred kilos lighter.

And what he was really surprised about what

how Matt didn't look outraged, shocked or anything like that. He honestly looked okay with it.

"You knew?" Josh asked.

Josh didn't really want to look at Matt when he answered so he focused back on the menu and looked at the vegan dishes. He was still getting his appetite back from the university social and eating an animal was the last thing he wanted.

"Yep. I knew I sort of guessed you liked me. I'm sorry I didn't tell you about Alice sooner," Matt said. "But why did it play on your mind so much?"

Josh focused on a vegan pizza that he had no intention of eating because he much preferred the vegan pies here. But he didn't want to look at Matt.

"My past. You probably don't know being bi but I haven't had it easier being gay. My family is homophobic, my friends hated me for ages and I'm had more abuse thrown at me than I know what to do with,"

"And you thought I was a new beginning for you," Matt said.

Damn this man was hot.

Josh wanted so badly to kiss, love and hug Matt, and it was so great to have someone else he actually sounded like they understood what you went through. It was just a shame that they could never be together.

"Why me though?" Matt asked.

Josh couldn't even understand why he would ask that. It was clear why anyone would ask him out.

"You're confused?" Matt asked.

"Well yea. You're beautiful, kind and an amazing guy," Josh said.

As soon as the words left his mouth he just wanted the ground to swollen him up. He never should have called a guy beautiful on a first non-official date or ever for that matter.

Josh stood up. "Thanks for this but-"

Matt grabbed his hand. "It's fine. Really. Stay,"

"Matt!" Alice shouted. "Gay boy get away from my boyfriend!"

Josh looked at a steaming furious Alice storm through the crowd of sporty men towards him and Tilly tried to slow her down and Beth just grabbed Josh.

Josh didn't know what was happening.

But Tilly and Beth grabbed Josh and pulled him away.

As Josh fainted from sheer stress all he heard was Alice screaming and shouting at Matt.

Josh couldn't believe what he had done to his beautiful Matt.

CHAPTER 12
19th June 2022
Canterbury, England

"Why the fuck would you do that!" Alice shouted.

At this point Matt really couldn't care less about Alice and her rage towards him. All he had been trying to do as they walked along a very quiet high street with the smooth cobblestones under their feet, was to be a good person.

Alice would never understand what it was like for gay and bisexual people to discover themselves, and all the utter crap they had to deal with. And tonight Alice was certainly adding to that crap.

Matt had little clue how she had found out but it was clear that Alice had probably questioned why Beth was with us and not with the so-called "loser" Josh, but he wasn't a loser.

He was far from it.

Josh was an amazingly hot sexy guy that cared

about him and actually wanted to connect with Matt. Alice hadn't wanted that for so long and she had never cared about his past experiences, how he actually was and most importantly his ideas about having kids.

But he still liked her and he had always been clear on that front.

"Matt!"

"What do you want from me!" Matt shouted as he spun around to face Alice.

She looked so furious and mad and like she was going to hit him, but her frown only got thinner and thinner. And Matt was seriously starting to wonder why he had ever been with her in the first place.

Whenever Josh had spoken to Matt, it was like Matt was the only person in the entire world and Matt was someone so important that josh would defend him to the end. Matt honestly couldn't remember a time when Alice had made him feel like that.

"I want you to explain yourself. Why are you cheating on me?" Alice asked.

Matt just laughed. It was ridiculous that she believed he was cheating on her. At the end of the day it was Matt who had always loved her, had sex with her and reassured her constantly how much he… liked her.

It just dawned on Matt that he had never said he actually loved her to her face.

"I'm not cheating on you," Matt said as he started slowly walking down the high street again.

"I don't believe you. You and that boy text each other when I'm sleeping. How long has this been going on?"

Matt just laughed because all of this was so ridiculous. He had never given her a reason to doubt him before, so why couldn't she just trust him now?

"He texted me yes. He really likes me, yes. Did he want to ask me out? Yes," Matt said.

Matt almost laughed again and the absolutely furious face that Alice was twisting into, but he forced himself not to.

Instead he simply stopped walking and gently hugged this very nice woman that he really liked, but didn't love.

"I don't want you ever seeing him again," Alice said coldly.

"You can't tell me what to do and live my life. Too many people have done that before to me and Josh. No more," Matt said dangerously calm.

Matt had no clue where all that anger had come from but it was probably from the fact that when him and Josh had been sitting there together, Josh had reminded him of his own rubbish childhood and his quest to become bi.

A journey he would never want for anyone else, but he never wanted his journey to go away. It was a part of him now and Josh understood that. Matt just knew he did.

And Alice did not.

Alice smiled and wrapped her little arms around

Matt and started kissing him. Matt had seen Alice do this before after fights and it was her way of manipulating him and making him forget their fights.

But he was so done with people that wanted to manipulate him and control who he was and how he lived.

"Goodbye Alice," Matt said walking away.

"Fine then have your fucking fairy boyfriend! You suck at sex anyway!" Alice shouted.

Matt just smiled because it was actually her that sucked at sex. Definitely not Matt.

CHAPTER 13
19th June 2022
Rochester, England

Josh was actually rather surprised at how great, amazing and funny Tilly was as the three of them got back into his parent's house and took him upstairs.

The car ride over was a bit hazy and Josh felt so ill that he almost couldn't think straight (not that he wanted to be thinking straight anyway).

As the two girls got Josh on the bed and helped him up so he was sitting as straight as his body allowed him to, Josh couldn't believe how his life was going at the moment. Two days ago he had been happy, excited and seriously looking forward to the amazing possible future of him and Matt being together.

But now he was just a silly pathetic man with a massive headache with it constantly corkscrewing through his mind. It wasn't exactly helpful but thankfully Beth had got downstairs, gotten some glasses of water and turned the lights on.

Josh realised he seriously needed to tidy up his bedroom. His bedding was all over the floor, his desk was a mess and even his curtains looked so sad from not being opened for a while.

"I didn't think you liked me," Josh said to Tilly.

Tilly looked so confused by the question.

"Dearest Josh," Tilly said "I've always liked you. You're a great student, funny and Matt likes you more than he ever wants to admit,"

Even those words made Josh feel like he had been punched in the stomach and now he felt even worse. He easily could have had a chance with Matt but he had been about a year too late.

"And dearest Josh, if you make Matt happy then I will only help that,"

"But I thought you liked Alice and were like best friends," Josh said as another wave of his headache washed over him.

"No not really. She's nice and all but Matt has never said he loved her and I don't blame him," Tilly said.

Josh pulled up his bedsheets over himself tighter. He needed to feel protected and comfortable at least after the craziness of the past two days. Then he would decide what needed to happen next.

"How did Alice find out about me and Matt going out?"

"Not on a date," Tilly said firmly but with a slight smile.

Josh just pulled her a funny face.

"Alice found it strange darling that I wasn't with you, and Matt wasn't there either," Beth said. "So she started searching the bars and restaurants and we were getting so many looks by security that we just had to tell her,"

"Sorry," Tilly and Beth said.

Even though he always knew that Beth would be sorry for ever hurting him. It still took him by surprise because he hadn't had anyone feel sorry, bad or anything like that for him for ages.

"Did you at least get anything out of it?" Beth asked.

Josh shrugged. "We connected. I said I liked him and I had wanted to ask him out and I told him a bit about my past,"

Beth hissed.

"What?" Josh asked as he sat up deadly straight in his bed.

"Darling you don't just tell a guy that on the first non-official date," Beth said looking at Tilly. "Knowing about your abuse is a turn-off for most guys,"

Of course. Josh was such an idiot, and now because he was so desperate he had probably blown it with the only guy that might have loved him. He was definitely going to die alone, unloved and unremembered.

"Wait abuse?" Tilly asked.

"No offense but I'll not talk about it tonight,"

Josh said rolling over and trying to get under the covers.

"That's fine, but Matt suffered his fair share of abuse as he came out as Bi. His family… mixed to say the least. He lost a few friends and more," Tilly said.

Josh just looked at her and uncovered some of the bedsheet as if he was gesturing her to join him. She just laughed slightly.

Beth folded her arms. "What we gonna do now about Matt?"

Josh shrugged. He needed sleep that was for sure but he had a feeling that he needed to have another conversation with Matt.

The lucky thing was as tomorrow was Monday and PhD students hadn't finished yet completely. Matt would be at the university and maybe Josh could find him and finish off their conversation tomorrow.

Even if he was still with Alice (which he oddly hoped he was) Josh could at least thank him for last night because he made an effort.

The first guy to ever make an effort where Josh was concerned.

PART THREE: REPAIRING A BROKEN HEART

BREAKING, NURSING, REPAIRING A BROKEN HEART

CHAPTER 14
20th June 2022
Canterbury, England

Probably the hardest thing about doing a PhD was the meetings and all the endless amounts of revision and rewriting that Matt had to do before he moved onto the next stage. It certainly wasn't his idea of fun but given how this was only his first year of doing his PhD, he just really hoped that it would be easier next year.

Matt closed Graham's office door and he was so glad to get out of that office, because as great as Graham was. He seriously needed to change his lunch order of a curry sandwich. It might have been extremely nice but it did stink the office out, and it was definitely not a fun place to sit in for two hours.

And Matt had really hoped his nose would get used to it over time, but that wasn't happening in the slightest at the moment.

"Matt," Josh said.

Matt looked all the way down the long university corridor with its wooden walls that were covered in all sorts of posters, billboards and other announcements, and Matt just smiled when he saw beautiful Josh walk towards him.

Matt was a little surprised with himself that he didn't feel any anger, disappointment or upset because technically Josh had cost him a relationship with Alice.

But as Josh walked towards him wearing a pair of denim shorts that revealed his stunning legs, a wonderful t-shirt that revealed just how fit and sexy he really was and Josh's handsome youthful face was framed perfectly. Matt really didn't care.

Josh was definitely a lot more beautiful, sexy and stunning than Alice, and there was definitely more of a connection between them. But Matt couldn't understand why Josh was here on the first official day of the university break.

Hell he was wondering why *he* was here at all. Graham had wanted to do the meeting in September but Matt was always the good student.

Josh stopped in front of Matt and for some strange reason extended his hand but Matt just smiled. Surely they were past that stage after the past few days.

Matt grabbed Josh's amazingly smooth hand and hugged him tight. Matt loved the sheer amount of love, chemistry and affection that flooded them both, and Matt seriously never wanted this to end.

After a few seconds Josh tried to walk away but Matt just wanted to hug a little longer. Then it dawned on him that Josh did actually want to get away so he quickly released him and took a few steps back.

"Wait. What about Alice?" Josh asked, looking around like he had just done the worse thing imaginable.

Matt shrugged. "We broke up. She wanted me to stop seeing you as a friend. I said I no longer wanted people to control my life and we broke up,"

Josh smiled for a moment then frowned. He really frowned.

Matt took a few steps closer to him and gently took Josh's hand in his.

"What's wrong?" Matt asked.

He honestly couldn't figure out why Josh would be sad or just put-off by that. Surely it was what they both wanted, Josh would now ask him out and they would date to see if what they had was real.

What was wrong with that?

Josh looked to the floor. "You know I said about my past and the abuse,"

Matt nodded.

"One of the pieces of my past was that a boy broke up with his girlfriend, his parents were mad, his friends hated him and it destroyed his life all for me. There was too much hate for a relationship to happen. I can't do that to you,"

Matt smiled. That was the most rubbish he had

ever heard. He wasn't going to hate or dislike Josh for something that his girlfriend had done.

And it wasn't like his parents or friends were going to take it out on Josh, no matter what Alice might tell them.

Matt gestured them to walk and Josh slowly nodded but he didn't dare look at Matt.

"I don't hate you," Matt said.

Josh nodded. "It's not you I'm worried about. A relationship requires support. Are you telling me your parents and friends would be happy that a heartbreaker like me entered their lives? Especially with how great Alice was meant to be,"

Matt didn't know what to say. Josh had a good point about his family and friends loving Alice because she loved Matt, she was good to him and they all respected her.

Josh laughed. "Exactly,"

Matt wanted to say something but he couldn't find the right words.

Josh took Matt's hands in his. "You deserve someone better than me,"

Josh kissed Matt's cheek and then he simply walked away.

Matt wanted to run after him and tell him that he loved Josh and he didn't care what anyone else thought about them.

But he couldn't move. He just felt like he was watching the love of his life walk away from him and there was nothing he could do to stop it.

CHAPTER 15
20th June 2022
Rochester, England

"So you broke up with a guy because you were scared?" Beth asked.

Josh was hardly impressed himself when Beth put it like that as they walked about the immensely long Rochester High Street with its perfectly smooth cobblestone road, little Victorian shops with the massive cathedral in the background.

"No I wasn't scared," Josh said.

But both him and Beth just knew he was lying completely. He had driven down to Canterbury that morning with such amazing hopes about possibly continuing their talk, being friends and just finally being himself. But as Matt told him about the breakup and everything else that would probably happen, he got scared.

Josh moved out the way as a young family walked down the high street, and Josh looked at Beth.

"I've screwed up haven't I?" Josh asked.

Beth laughed and stopped outside a very old candy shop that sold all the old sweets that you couldn't buy in the supermarkets anymore.

"Definitely darling," Beth said. "You had your chance to be with a beautiful man and you blew it,"

Josh hated how this was going. He just didn't want Matt to go through all the emotional pain that the guy from his past did. It was ridiculous and silly that Matt was too good for him anyway.

All he wanted to do was protect Matt.

"The real question is how are you going to fix it," Beth said as she gestured they should go into the candy shop.

Josh rolled his eyes and went in first.

Josh loved the amazing smell of sugar, sweets and chocolate as him and Beth went into the little shop with rows upon rows of jars filled with sweets, and a very elderly woman behind the counter.

The elderly woman waved at Beth and Josh was seriously starting to wonder how often Beth came in here.

"Maybe I shouldn't fix it," Josh said. "Maybe I should leave the university and transfer and to another. That way I can still do my degree and Matt can focus on his PhD without thinking or running into me,"

Beth rolled her eyes. "Seriously? That is just utter rubbish. You need to talk to him and-"

"Isn't talking to Matt how I got him into this

mess? Because of me of his friends and family will be so disappointed that Alice is gone, they all loved her and now I'm going to be known as the heartbreaker in the family. How the hell are me and Matt meant to have a relationship if they think that of me?"

Josh ran his fingers over a row of jars of different flavours of sherbet, something he normally hated but he wasn't exactly in the mood for something he liked. Especially with his parents having to take the day off work to go to their grandparents again because there was another emergency.

Beth picked up a large jar of chocolate covered coffee beans and took it over to the counter.

"Four bags please," Beth said.

Josh didn't know if the elderly woman was going to faint or something, but after a few moments she took out four little paper bags and filled them up with the chocolate coffee beans.

"How do you honestly know that's what his family will think of you? Tilly likes you and surely the rest of his friends and family will after they get a chance to know you," Beth said.

Josh supposed she had a good point but he still didn't want Matt going through any of the emotional pain that the other boy did from his past. That pain and hate from his friends and family had almost destroyed that boy and then the boy had turned the hate and everything on Josh.

He didn't want to experience that ever again. It was too much of a risk.

He had to get away. Josh just had to leave the university, go to a new one and restart his romantic life.

It was the only way to spare Matt all the feelings Josh wasn't able to spare the people from his past.

Beth offered Josh one of the bags of chocolate coffee beans, Josh simply shook his head and walked away.

He had a lot of planning to do for his new future.

CHAPTER 16
20th June 2022
Canterbury, England

Even though he had broken up with Alice about a day ago, Matt still couldn't believe how great it felt to have a bed all to himself. It was going to be amazing to have a peaceful night sleep without any snoring, moaning or constant demands for bad sex.

This was going to be amazing.

Matt laid in his large double bed watching a film on his laptop as he tried to get to sleep with only his boxers on. Of course he knew from his psychology classes that the blue light coming off the laptop was hardly going to help but he didn't really care at this point.

The sound of the doorbell going so late at night made Matt pause the film because it was slightly beyond strange for someone wanting to come here tonight. But after a few moments Matt just ignored it, it was probably something for his parents.

Matt had wanted to spend tonight talking, laughing and joking with sexy Josh about life with them going on their first date. That would have made his day, week and year. Matt really wanted nothing else than to be with Josh.

Yet it turned out that Josh had stopped taking his calls and wasn't replying to any texts or emails that he spent.

Matt sort of understood Josh's concerns and it was really sweet of him to worry so much about him and his feelings. But Matt really, really wanted to be with Josh no matter what his parents and friends thought.

Tilly had already called him today to ask if he was going and when his and Josh's first date was. For some reason as much as Matt loved the call, he felt so emotional, raw and strange because it was something he wanted so badly but he was never going to get it.

Two pairs of footsteps came up the stairs.

Matt closed his laptop and it was strange that his parents would both come up to see him. There was no one else it could possibly be.

His bedroom door opened and Matt really wished he was wearing something to cover his chest and legs.

Tilly and Beth walked in and they didn't even seem to pay attention to the fact he was basically naked.

"You need to go and see Josh," Beth said firmly. Tilly nodded.

"Why? What's wrong?" Matt said sitting up straight.

Beth and Tilly both walked around his bed and sat on opposite sides of him.

"Josh is slightly beyond bad dearest," Tilly said. "He wants to change university, spare you pain and basically make sure you never have to see him again,"

Matt couldn't believe that. He never ever wanted Josh to move away. Matt wanted to see Josh for the rest of his life, he needed, wanted him.

"What would I say? I can't change his mind. He couldn't listen to me," Matt said.

"Gays and Bisexuals are pain in the butts," Tilly said.

Beth laughed. "Seriously Matt. Put some clothes on. I would recommend you at least trim your chest a little but we don't have time. And we need to take you to Josh's house like now before he ruins his life,"

Matt was slightly embarrassed that they had both noticed he was basically naked, but they were right. Completely.

He had to get his act together and race against time to save the man he loved from himself.

CHAPTER 17
20th June 2022
Rochester, England

Matt flat out couldn't believe he was actually going to do this crazy thing. Tilly and Beth and him had driven for a half hour to get to Rochester and they had just parked outside. Matt felt his stomach churn, his palms turn clammy and he just didn't know what to say.

"Go on then," Tilly and Beth said.

Knowing better than to argue with his best friend and Beth (that was quickly turning into another great friend), he slowly got out of the car. And was rather impressed with the large white house in front of him with a wonderful rose garden to his left, a very expensive car to his right and an amazing granite pathway leading up to a large black front door.

Matt slowly walked up to the door. He had no clue what he was going to say, and it would be a million times worse if Josh's parents answered because then Matt would actually have to talk to them too. He didn't want to do that.

He wasn't sure he wanted to do any of this.

The night was delightfully cool, not too hot and definitely not too cold for a summer night with the street lights weakly illuminating the street.

Matt reached the front door and tapped on the door quietly. He didn't want to do this, he was too scared as well. He was scared about breaking Josh's heart all over again and only adding to his emotional past.

Matt didn't want Josh to live in a world where he only saw failed relationships and possibilities. Matt really wanted to help him realise that being gay was a path to happiness, love and amazing wonders that the two of them could only dream of.

But only if they were together.

Matt knocked on the door hard.

No one came to the door so Matt banged on the door even harder.

Matt heard the door unlock and Josh's amazing handsome beautiful face popped round. Josh smiled for a brief second then went to shut the door.

Matt grabbed the front door. He wasn't going to let Josh run away from him without Matt at least getting a chance to tell him how he felt.

"Don't go," Matt said. "I need you. I care about you. I want to be with you,"

Josh weakly smiled. "You're out of my league and you deserve to be with someone better than a guy like me,"

"Fuck off," Matt said. "I don't care what league you think you're in. I don't care what you think I deserve. Let me decide for once in both our lives what I actually want from my own life,"

Josh looked up and Matt just stared into his amazing wonderful eyes.

"All I have ever wanted," Matt said, "was an amazing caring person that actually loved me. I thought I had that with Alice but I didn't. She was just like the rest of them in the end, but you actually don't care that I'm bi and you want me to be happy,"

Josh nodded.

Matt took both of Josh's hands in his.

"Well," Matt said, "you make me happy,"

Josh slowly opened the door fully and Matt took him in his arms. Matt and Josh both slowly kissed each other's soft smooth lips and their hands gently explored the backs of each other.

Matt flat out loved the sheer chemistry, affection and love that flowed between them, and as his wayward parts flared to life. Matt realised this was going to be the start of something truly amazing.

For too long he had suffered in silence and had just been expected to play by the rules of others. Like acting straight, getting a great girlfriend and only doing all that straight stuff.

Matt had never truly explored what being bi meant. He had thought it was just liking both men and women, but it wasn't. It was about finding what truly made you happy in a moment in time.

Sometimes women had definitely made Matt happy, other times it had certainly been men. But as Matt continued kissing the gorgeous man in front of him, Matt just knew that he was going to be happy with Josh forever.

It was just a feeling and a feeling that Matt was always going to treasure, protect and adore. Because after everything both of them had experienced, it was Josh that made him truly happy.

And that was worth the world to Matt.

CHAPTER 18
21st June 2022
Rochester, England

Josh had to admit that his small single bed definitely wasn't perfect for two people sleeping together and having sex in, but thankfully Josh and Matt had managed perfectly. And it really had been a magical night.

Josh laid on his single bed with Matt's amazingly smooth great-looking arms wrapped around him as he slept. Josh still had to admit that he normally wasn't a fan of men with hairy chests but Matt's was growing on him, and he just really liked (and probably loved) Matt.

Matt was kind, amazing and just such a wonderful person. And he was so, so warm in bed. Before last night Josh had no idea what it felt like to have another person in bed with him.

It felt amazing.

Little slivers of light shone into the bedroom and

Josh was definitely going to open the curtains sooner or later. Because this wasn't about hiding from the world anymore, it was all about experiencing new things, being himself and living life.

As Josh watched Matt's stunningly handsome face sleep, Josh just wanted to kiss him because he was truly lucky to have someone so special in his life.

And Josh finally felt as if it was finally dealing with his past. For it was just that, the past, for all the bullying, the torment and the pain that other people had inflicted on Josh, all those people were gone and they could never hurt him again.

Josh had realised last night as Matt had fallen asleep that he didn't need to carry all that weight and baggage around with him anymore. All he really needed was an amazing wonderful man that only cared about him and the future.

Thankfully they were the same. Josh didn't have a shadow of a doubt that him and Matt would be together for years to come and hopefully forever, something that Josh hardly minded.

The wonderful smell of crispy bacon, eggs and warming toast filled the bedroom and Josh listened to the stomping of his parents downstairs. He was so glad to finally have them back after all the drama with his grandparents and they were keeping it from him.

Josh's parents had texted him last night about it all and it turned out that his grandparents had been struggling with their health for a while, and now they had decided to move them into a home.

Josh was actually okay about that, because as much as he loved them and knew that them being in a home wasn't ideal. It was what they needed and he could always visit them, and thankfully the homes around Rochester were rather good.

So they would still be around for a long time to come.

And Josh supposed that he was actually rather glad that his parents had kept it from him. Because with all the things with Matt going on he didn't need the extra stress, worry and concern about his grandparents, and that was why his parents were truly amazing.

They always knew what to and not say to him until the time was right.

Granted he had absolutely no clue how he was going to introduce or explain to them why he had a sexy man in his bed a few days after Josh had told them him and Matt could never be together.

But Josh just knew they would be fine with it in the end. They might have still been getting used to the fact he was gay and having a gay sex life (at least he actually had one after last night) but he knew they truly loved him.

Matt finally stirred, smiled and kissed Josh on the lips, and Josh really didn't know if he was ever going to get used to those amazingly soft velvety lips that he loved so much.

Then Josh heard his mum stomp up the stairs (not because she was angry, it was just how she walked) and Josh's stomach flipped with butterflies as the most important people in his life were actually going to meet.

Matt gave Josh another kiss, they both threw some clothes on then they went downstairs, hand in hand to start the next amazing chapter of their life together, because that was what they were.

They were always going to be two amazing people in love who treasured each other and never ever wanted to be without the other.

And that was just perfect to Josh and he just knew that Matt felt the exact same way.

GET YOUR FREE AND EXCLUSIVE SHORT STORY NOW! LEARN ABOUT NEMESIO'S PAST!

https://www.subscribepage.com/fireheart

BREAKING, NURSING, REPAIRING A BROKEN HEART

Keep up to date with exclusive deals on Connor Whiteley's Books, as well as the latest news about new releases and so much more!

Sign up for the Grab a Book and Chill Monthly newsletter, and you'll get one **FREE** ebook just for signing up: Agents of The Emperor Collection.

Sign Up Now!

https://dl.bookfunnel.com/f4p5xkprbk

About the author:

Connor Whiteley is the author of over 60 books in the sci-fi fantasy, nonfiction psychology and books for writer's genre and he is a Human Branding Speaker and Consultant.

He is a passionate warhammer 40,000 reader, psychology student and author.

Who narrates his own audiobooks and he hosts The Psychology World Podcast.

All whilst studying Psychology at the University of Kent, England.

Also, he was a former Explorer Scout where he gave a speech to the Maltese President in August 2018 and he attended Prince Charles' 70th Birthday Party at Buckingham Palace in May 2018.

Plus, he is a self-confessed coffee lover!

OTHER SHORT STORIES BY CONNOR WHITELEY

<u>Mystery Short Stories:</u>
Our Woman In Paris
Corrupt Driving
A Prime Assassination
Jubilee Thief
Jubilee, Terror, Celebrations
Negative Jubilation
Ghostly Jubilation
Killing For Womenkind
A Snowy Death
Miracle Of Death
A Spy In Rome
The 12:30 To St Pancreas
A Country In Trouble
A Smokey Way To Go
A Spicy Way To GO
A Marketing Way To Go
A Missing Way To Go
A Showering Way To Go
Poison In The Candy Cane
Christmas Innocence
You Better Watch Out
Christmas Theft
Trouble In Christmas
Smell of The Lake

Problem In A Car
Theft, Past and Team
Embezzler In The Room
A Strange Way To Go
A Horrible Way To Go
Ann Awful Way To Go
An Old Way To Go
A Fishy Way To Go
A Pointy Way To Go
A High Way To Go
A Fiery Way To Go
A Glassy Way To Go
A Chocolatey Way To Go
Kendra Detective Mystery Collection Volume 1
Kendra Detective Mystery Collection Volume 2
Stealing A Chance At Freedom
Glassblowing and Death
Theft of Independence
Cookie Thief
Marble Thief
Book Thief
Art Thief
Mated At The Morgue
The Big Five Whoopee Moments
Stealing An Election

BREAKING, NURSING, REPAIRING A BROKEN HEART

Mystery Short Story Collection Volume 1
Mystery Short Story Collection Volume 2
Criminal Performance

<u>Science Fiction Short Stories:</u>
Vigil
Emperor Forgive Us
Their Brave New World
Gummy Bear Detective
The Candy Detective
What Candies Fear
The Blurred Image
Shattered Legions
The First Rememberer
Life of A Rememberer
System of Wonder
Lifesaver
Remarkable Way She Died
The Interrogation of Annabella Stormic
Blade of The Emperor
Arbiter's Truth
Computation of Battle
Old One's Wrath
Puppets and Masters
Ship of Plague
Interrogation
Edge of Failure

One Way Choice
Acceptable Losses
Balance of Power
Good Idea At The Time
Escape Plan
Escape In The Hesitation
Inspiration In Need
Singing Warriors
Knowledge is Power
Killer of Polluters
Climate of Death
The Family Mailing Affair
Defining Criminality
The Martian Affair
A Cheating Affair
The Little Café Affair
Mountain of Death
Prisoner's Fight
Claws of Death
Bitter Air
Honey Hunt
Blade On A Train
<u>Fantasy Short Stories:</u>
City of Snow
City of Light
City of Vengeance
Dragons, Goats and Kingdom

BREAKING, NURSING, REPAIRING A BROKEN HEART

Smog The Pathetic Dragon
Don't Go In The Shed
The Tomato Saver
The Remarkable Way She Died
The Bloodied Rose
Asmodia's Wrath
Heart of A Killer
Emissary of Blood
Dragon Coins
Dragon Tea
Dragon Rider
Sacrifice of the Soul
Heart of The Flesheater
Heart of The Regent
Heart of The Standing
Feline of The Lost
Heart of The Story
City of Fire
Awaiting Death

Other books by Connor Whiteley:

Bettie English Private Eye Series
A Very Private Woman
The Russian Case
A Very Urgent Matter
A Case Most Personal
Trains, Scots and Private Eyes
The Federation Protects

Lord of War Origin Trilogy:
Not Scared Of The Dark
Madness
Burn It All

The Fireheart Fantasy Series
Heart of Fire
Heart of Lies
Heart of Prophecy
Heart of Bones
Heart of Fate

City of Assassins (Urban Fantasy)
City of Death
City of Marytrs
City of Pleasure
City of Power

Agents of The Emperor
Return of The Ancient Ones
Vigilance
Angels of Fire
Kingmaker
The Eight
The Lost Generation
Lord Of War Trilogy (Agents of The Emperor)
Not Scared Of The Dark
Madness
Burn It All Down

The Garro Series- Fantasy/Sci-fi
GARRO: GALAXY'S END
GARRO: RISE OF THE ORDER
GARRO: END TIMES
GARRO: SHORT STORIES
GARRO: COLLECTION
GARRO: HERESY
GARRO: FAITHLESS
GARRO: DESTROYER OF WORLDS
GARRO: COLLECTIONS BOOK 4-6
GARRO: MISTRESS OF BLOOD
GARRO: BEACON OF HOPE
GARRO: END OF DAYS

Winter Series- Fantasy Trilogy Books
WINTER'S COMING
WINTER'S HUNT
WINTER'S REVENGE
WINTER'S DISSENSION

Miscellaneous:
RETURN
FREEDOM
SALVATION
Reflection of Mount Flame
The Masked One
The Great Deer

Gay Romance Novellas
Breaking, Nursing, Repiaring A Broken Heart
Jacob And Daniel
Fallen For A Lie
His Heartstopper
Spying And Weddings

<u>All books in 'An Introductory Series':</u>
Careers In Psychology
Psychology of Suicide
Dementia Psychology
Forensic Psychology of Terrorism And Hostage-Taking
Forensic Psychology of False Allegations
Year In Psychology
<u>BIOLOGICAL PSYCHOLOGY 3RD EDITION</u>
<u>COGNITIVE PSYCHOLOGY THIRD EDITION</u>
<u>SOCIAL PSYCHOLOGY- 3RD EDITION</u>
<u>ABNORMAL PSYCHOLOGY 3RD EDITION</u>
<u>PSYCHOLOGY OF RELATIONSHIPS- 3RD EDITION</u>
<u>DEVELOPMENTAL PSYCHOLOGY 3RD EDITION</u>
<u>HEALTH PSYCHOLOGY</u>
<u>RESEARCH IN PSYCHOLOGY</u>
<u>A GUIDE TO MENTAL HEALTH AND TREATMENT AROUND THE WORLD- A GLOBAL LOOK AT DEPRESSION</u>
<u>FORENSIC PSYCHOLOGY</u>
<u>THE FORENSIC PSYCHOLOGY OF THEFT, BURGLARY AND OTHER</u>

CRIMES AGAINST PROPERTY
CRIMINAL PROFILING: A FORENSIC PSYCHOLOGY GUIDE TO FBI PROFILING AND GEOGRAPHICAL AND STATISTICAL PROFILING.
CLINICAL PSYCHOLOGY
FORMULATION IN PSYCHOTHERAPY
PERSONALITY PSYCHOLOGY AND INDIVIDUAL DIFFERENCES
CLINICAL PSYCHOLOGY REFLECTIONS VOLUME 1
CLINICAL PSYCHOLOGY REFLECTIONS VOLUME 2
Clinical Psychology Reflections Volume 3
CULT PSYCHOLOGY
Police Psychology

A Psychology Student's Guide To University
How Does University Work?
A Student's Guide To University And Learning
University Mental Health and Mindset

www.ingramcontent.com/pod-product-compliance
Lightning Source LLC
LaVergne TN
LVHW011846060526
838200LV00054B/4181